CHELTENHAM

Cheltenham Festivals is the charitable organisation which organises the internationally acclaimed Jazz, Science, Music and Literature Festivals. Through cutting-edge and creative programming, Cheltenham's four inspirational festivals have been at the forefront of the UK's cultural scene since the inaugural Music Festival in 1945.

By championing the best up-and-coming young talent, celebrating the work of established artists and commissioning unique and surprising performances, Cheltenham Festivals enriches the cultural lives of its audiences. Schools, young people and our local community can enjoy the Festivals year round through our extensive programme of educational workshops, talks, projects and inspiring activities.

For more information and details of how to support Cheltenham Festivals, see www.cheltenhamfestivals.com.

FIRST STORY

First Story is a charity that aims to celebrate and foster creativity, literacy and talent in young people. We're cheerleaders for books, stories, reading and writing. We've seen how creative writing can build students' self-esteem and aspirations.

We place acclaimed authors as writers-in-residence in state schools across the country. Each author leads weekly after-school workshops for up to twenty-one students. We publish the students' work in anthologies and arrange public readings and book launches at which the students can read aloud to friends, families and teachers.

For more information and details of how to support First Story, see www.firststory.org.uk or contact us at info@firststory.org.uk.

Some of These Things Are True
ISBN 978-0-85748-167-2

Published in Great Britain by
First Story Limited · Sixth Floor · 2 Seething Lane
London EC3N 4AT
www.firststory.org.uk
in partnership with
Cheltenham Festivals · 109–111 Bath Road
Cheltenham GL53 7LS
www.cheltenhamfestivals.com

Copyright © First Story 2015

Typesetter: Avon DataSet Ltd
Cover Illustration: Aimée Sullivan
Cover Designer: Brett Evans Biedscheid
Printed in the UK by Intype Libra Ltd

Cheltenham Festivals is a registered charity number 251765.

First Story is a registered charity number 1122939 and a private company limited by guarantee
incorporated in England with number 06487410. First Story is a business name of First Story Limited.

Some of These Things Are True

An Anthology

By The Cheltenham Festivals First Story Group
At All Saints' Academy

Edited and introduced by Cliff Yates | 2015

CHELTENHAMFESTIVALS

FIRST STORY
Creativity Literacy Confidence

As Patron of First Story I am delighted that it continues to foster and inspire the creativity and talent of young people in challenging secondary schools.

I firmly believe that nurturing a passion for reading and writing is vital to the health of our country. I am therefore greatly encouraged to know that young people in this school – and across the country – have been meeting each week throughout the year in order to write together.

I send my warmest congratulations to everybody who is published in this anthology.

Camilla

HRH The Duchess of Cornwall

Thank You

The Hitchins Family Trust within the **Gloucestershire Community Foundation** and the **Wates Foundation**.

Melanie Curtis at **Avon DataSet** for her overwhelming support for First Story and for giving her time in typesetting this anthology.

Anna Wood for her meticulous copy-editing and her enthusiastic support for the project.

The **University of Gloucestershire** Illustration Department for their support for Cheltenham Festivals First Story, and **Aimée Sullivan** in particular for giving her time to illustrate the cover of this anthology.

Brett Evans Biedscheid for designing the cover of this anthology.

Intype Libra for printing this anthology at a discounted rate, **Tony Chapman** and **Moya Birchall** at Intype Libra for their advice.

The Wilson Cheltenham Art Gallery and Museum.

Most importantly we would like to thank the students, teachers and writers who have worked so hard to make First Story a success this year, as well as the many individuals and organisations (including those who we may have omitted to name) who have given their generous time, support and advice.

Contents

Introduction

Cliff Yates

WRITER-IN-RESIDENCE

All the work in this anthology was written by students at All Saints' Academy in Cheltenham who met with me for workshops from September 2014 to March 2015. Our workshops took place after school on Friday afternoons. Young people have busy lives, both in and out of school, so to stay behind for a writing group on Friday afternoons shows an impressive commitment to writing.

What really impressed me was the supportive atmosphere in the group and their willingness to share their work with each other, right from the very first session, even when writing about something that was personal to them. It felt like a privilege to be there. The students' concentration and focus was excellent. During the workshop that took place during our visit to The Wilson Art Gallery & Museum, for example, they carried on writing as if there was no one else in the room, even with a photographer filming them over their shoulders; I'm not sure that many adult writers would have been able to manage that. Another thing that impressed me, throughout the sessions, was the students' enthusiasm for writing and their receptiveness to new ideas. Some of them, for example, had not written poems since primary school. Halfway through the first session, however, they were writing poems as if they'd been writing them for years.

Some workshop exercises involved writing about memories, some involved writing fiction, and some involved writing about imaginary things as if they were true. The title of our anthology is a fragment of a quotation from the novelist Hilary Mantel, who wrote in *Wolf Hall*: 'Some of these things are true and some of them lies. But they are all good stories.' The title can be seen as a kind of warning to the reader of this anthology: even things which are written as if they could could be true, might not be. All writing, including autobiography, is an act of the imagination. I also used 'some of these things are true' for a particular exercise, inspired by a poem by Angela France, where students had to write a list poem in which some of the things are true and some are not. The interesting thing about these poems, of course, is that it's sometimes hard to tell what is true and what is invented. The approach of using poems as springboards for the students' writing was important; we read poems by a wide range of poets, including Miroslav Holub, Jackie Wills, Matthew Sweeney and Raymond Carver.

It was a real pleasure to work with the students at All Saints' Academy, to witness the growth in their confidence and the progress in their writing. I hope that you enjoy reading their work as much as I did. This was the first time that Cheltenham Festivals and First Story have joined together to work with schools in Gloucestershire – long may their partnership continue.

Go and Open the Door

Eloise Taylor

Go and open that door.
Which door?
That door.

Go and open the door.
Push or pull?
Let's try push.
Oh wait – it was pull.

Quick, pause –
did anyone see that?
Carry on.

Go and open that door.
How can you expect me to touch
that germ-infested slab of wood?

Go and open that door.
There'll be wonders, you'll see!
No time to ponder,
listen for that bird.

Go and open that door
and please
don't lick the lamppost like the
last girl we had come through here.
We had trouble with that one.

Tiny Bird

Emily Bond

I remember the funny smell
that reminded me of the overpowering colour yellow.
I remember the whitewashed walls
which made me think of dreams.

I remember the room
with fluorescent stars
stuck to the ceiling.

I remember
the tubes going
in
and
out
of his body.

I remember
feeling afraid
to look at him,
to touch
his tiny arm.

Straight from the Bowl

Teresa Etheredge

I remember asking my mum for rice pudding.
Watching, bored, the royal wedding.
I remember melting chocolate with Caleb to eat straight from
    the bowl.
I remember the hard brown sofa we used to have and the soft
    cushions we still have.
I remember the tone of the telephone,
The scary voice asking me to try again later.

I remember eating from cardboard boxes in our new house,
When I tore my cheek in playgroup.
I remember a doctor with glasses sewing me up,
Receiving a toothbrush for being brave.
I remember a silky orange dress I wore, both liked and despised
    for liking.

I remember Paul jumping, arms outstretched toward the first
    monkey bar,
Laughing as he landed face-first.
I remember begging Mum for a parrot
And her lumpy custard –
True Ambrosia.

The day of the removal of two teeth.

The day, long-awaited, that I won at Scrabble,
My victory dance on the yellow sofa.
I remember being stopped by a policeman for pretending to
    steal jam,
Dyeing my hair green but
Crying when it washed out the next day.

I remember the blue cardigan from primary,
The holes under the arms.
I remember being told that my great-grandma died as I was
    born.
Sliding down the banister at our house in Wales,
Jumping from the stairs to touch the ceiling.

I wish I still needed to jump.

Multiverse

Asraf Khan

One Asraf isn't enough!
In another universe, far far away
He could be sat in school or even in space.
Earth may even be populated by a race comprised of only Asraf.
He might even be a she.
Am I his twin, or is he mine?

The Older Brother
I Never Had

Caitlin Leach

The older brother I never had
Would be short and dark-haired.
He'd wake me up for school
And give me bruises at breakfast.
He'd tell me about the girls he liked
Even though I'd never care,
I'd listen anyway
About how Dad likes me more
And I had it better at home.
He'd play sports
And always lose
But would thrive with video games.
He'd be a secret poet
And a secret mummy's boy.
He'd hate doing chores
And pay me to slave away after him.
I never would give in
And he never would really mind.
I'd listen to his favourite bands
And pretend they're better than mine.
I would cover his back for trying cigarettes
And he'd cover mine for mediocre grades.
I bet he would have a passion
For something bizarre

That I would try to copy
Because he's my older brother
And I'd love him
Like little sisters do.

A Blank Canvas

Jessica Knight

A long house
With vacant windows
And nothing but darkness.

The heavy staircase clunked
Under the sound of my feet.

The long corridor unfolded
Into a ghostly landing
Plastered with fine art and sickly wallpaper.

A four-poster bed lay useless in the bedroom
And a tiny bedside table with
Intricate Celtic patterns.

A small orange diary with a golden clasp
Closed tightly
With an easel close by
And a blank canvas
Left in a hurry.

The latch on the window was left open
Waiting for the purple sky
And the merciless wind
To consume the house.

Alice... Apparently

Bethany Halford

Well I woke up this morning
And I was someone I did not recognise
In a place that was ghastly... odd
With very odd people too.

I'm a girl,
Apparently.
Blonde hair and blue eyes
With black-and-white stockings. Why on earth would anyone
   wear them?

I like blue, I think.
I'm surrounded by a blue cat and caterpillar
They're oddly smiling.
I think I want to leave.

Oh dear,
Why am I crying?
I'm drowning in my tears.
How odd.

'What's your name?'
Oh gosh that wasn't the cat speaking,
Was it?
'Ummm.'

Fiction

Katie Cotton-Betteridge

If my life was imaginary,
Each action a word on a page,
Would it be Hermione, reading for my exams,
Smiling at each grade?
If I didn't really exist,
Which book would I be in?
Who would write about me?
Would they change anything about me?
What?
Would they write positively about me?
Why?
Which of my traits would they prefer?
How would they describe me,
The passion for my writing,
The way my nose crinkles in disgust?
If I was a fictional character,
Would the Doctor obsess over me?
Flinch at each mistake?
Shout when I'm happy?
If my life was imaginary
How would I know?

I Haven't Done Much in My Life

Casey Todd Hall

I haven't done much in my life, but there was this one time…
Walking up the fishy park with my bike and Dad,
His toolkit bouncing up and down in his hand.
Waiting patiently, ready to ride two wheels for the first time.
I sat down and was ready to go – complete on the first try,
Riding freely and on my own for the first time in forever.

Chinese Saturdays

Colbie McKinnon

I remember the strong scent of his vanilla incense sticks,
The cold nights tucked up warm in bed
Protected by Bob on my quilt.
I remember tripping up the narrow stairs,
Falling through his narrow halls.
His garden, overgrown yet peaceful,
Home to millions.
I remember the fear of frequent power-cuts
Then the realisation of the unpaid bills –
You wouldn't know at five.
Alien Scooby-Doo at midnight,
His old dusty Megadrive, Micro Machines and Bubsy,
Thousands of his Beatles albums
Displayed proudly on the whitewashed walls.
The video-store corner, a fond memory.
Chinese Saturdays,
Him burning his mouth on Kung Po.
I remember the single airbeds,
Little room for the four-poster
His princess deserved.
We didn't care.

Empty Patio Chairs

Meg Roberts

I ran upstairs to
number eleven.
I waited in
the paved back yard
buried in snow.
I sat down
with a patio chair in tow.
Greens, yellows, blue.
Fiery colour
filled the sky
as we sat
side by side
in the flurry of the snow.

My Nose Began to Bleed

Tim Justice

My nose began to gush.
I open my eyes to drops of dark red on the wooden floor.
I press my forehead and cry out for comfort.
My brother steps out of his room and peaks over the bannister.
As I look up, I see his hair like a yellow feather duster
glaring down at me as the tears roll down my cheeks.
A wave of steam hits me as my mother
opens the door to the kitchen in shock.
She horizontally walks over to the toilet
and wraps a roll of tissue and turns to me.
She lifts me to the second step with paper
gently resting on my nostrils.
After two minutes of pain, I slightly recover
and head back upstairs with an unnecessary limp.

A Vintage Armchair

Emily Bond

A vintage armchair
standing alone.
Its tartan check
reminds me of him.

A timeless study
stuffed full
of secondhand books.
Huge piles that almost
touch the ceiling.

A field in the
middle of nowhere.
The smell of manure.
I never will
understand why
you like it.

A purple tank top,
thick and slightly itchy.

A dusty radio
broadcasting

The Archers.

Seventy-two Hours

Asraf Khan

I remember eating all the cookies and denying it was me.
I remember the taste of salt in Weston during primary school –
The sea was blue, so I went for it.
I remember sitting in the dentist's chair.
I remember the heat of India.
I remember my laptop smoking.
I remember beating *Final Fantasy XIII* took me well over
    seventy-two hours.
I remember the sting of stinging nettles.
I remember saying my work got deleted.
I remember getting my white belt, and stopping.

I Hated Showers

Eloise Taylor

It was then I punched her in the face.
Cheater Beater, that's me.
Desperately wanting that cream-covered cake.
What with her moaning and screaming voice
Annoying others no end.
She's only a young 'un, my dad had said.
Cheese spread sandwiches
Faded blue dungarees
Rosy pinched cheeks
Naked dancing – always on the kitchen table.
Blow pens and *Doctor Who*
Ham and cheese baguettes
Dinner ladies with megaphones.
Racing towards that bright yellow fluff ball.
Meeting Archie for the first time,
Saying goodbye to Silas for the last.
Playing schools with my younger sister
Pretending we were on a plane.

How YOU Are a Superhero

Katie Cotton-Betteridge

Your palms sweat
your eyes sharpen
your legs shake
your hearing increases.
Adrenaline pumps through your body.
You hear the beat of your own heart,
taste the dirt in the air,
smell the sweat on the back of your neck.
You can run faster
your muscles get stronger
you can react quicker
your mind thinks better.
What you see negatively
is how you are a superhero.
What you see negatively
but makes you stronger than the rest.
Fear.

Try Not to Be

Teresa Etheredge

Now I'm on my own I can do what I want —
Watch the things we're not allowed to
With too many naughty words.
Play silly games until I get bored,
Complete all the levels, ignoring the spare remotes.
Cook gingerbread,
Decorate crazily,
Do secret things they don't know about.
Melt chocolate and stir in fudge,
Wrap up presents they're not allowed to see.
Go to town and wander round,
Peek in shops but buy nothing.

Choose what I want to watch
Or watch what they would have watched.
Listen to silence,
Listen to music.
Search random stuff.
Hoover. Clean.
Make it perfect for when they come back.
Try not to be lonely.

The Sister I Never Met

Jessica Knight

The sister I never met
Has jet black hair
A thin smile with slightly crooked teeth
And bright eyes that make everyone swoon.
She would cook dinner on Tuesdays
And read on Wednesdays.

We would walk together
Pointing out everything that came into view.
We would stop for coffee and
She'd always pay, no matter
How many times I offered.

She would teach me lessons I was
Yet to learn
And watch over me
But never treat me like a child.

This Is Temporary

Caitlin Leach

Trees bark
And zebras aren't real.
Drinking saltwater will clear pesky pimples.
The equator is invisible.

Dad can eat fire
And grass eats grass.
Breathing underwater won't kill you.
Sound is just vibrations.

Santa lives
And scars heal.
I won't let anyone hurt you.
Infinity has no end.

Socks run away
And words don't hurt.
Eating bread crust gives you curly hair.
Elephants never forget.

Money grows on trees
And the sky is blue.
Granny will live
Forever and forever.

Two Christmases

Meg Roberts

I hear the fizz of the Pepsi and whiskey
as Dad pours himself his third glass,
the sound of my grandparents Lyn and John
fussing over who didn't put out
the salt and pepper shakers.
The rustle of paper as
Charlie scores a slam-dunk into
the black binliner.
Our dog Amber growls playfully
as she challenges the men in the house.
The sound of my mother, Kate,
dishing the food up.
The muffled cries from Henrietta
as Heidi tries to get her to sleep
from behind the closed door.
The sound of Dougie's pattering feet
as he follows me through the
dining room door.
I hear the sound of my grandparents
Alice and Jack, in my ear saying
'Well done' and 'Merry Christmas'.

Rushing to Catch the Underground

Casey Todd Hall

I remember my sister telling me to wake up.
I remember missing to get dressed to catch the bus.
I remember the sigh of relief that I was finally on my way.
I remember people rushing to catch the underground.
I remember the laughter and the screams of excitement.
I remember seeing their faces – Jesse, Jeana and Louis Cole
for the first time ever, a dream come true.
I remember running to catch the coach but missing it.
I remember framing the autographs on my wall.
I remember watching the footage back of the day
and seeing the present they received.

Nanny Quacky

Colbie McKinnon

The nanny I never met was dinky at four foot
And made my little nan look like a giant
Her snow-like hair transformed from autumn's auburn.
And Scamp who lives in the outdoor shed
A ripe age of twenty-one.
A homely woman
She lives in a two-up-two-down in Leckhampton
Inviting my mum round every Saturday.

We call her Nanny Quacky.
There's no technical story behind this.
She called everyone Ducky.
It's funny, mum says she would have adored me.
I doubt it. I hope so.
A nanny's girl even through her teenage years.
She would serve bowls of custard and cream
Watching *Bagpuss* with mum
Or taking her to the abbey I remembered when I was two.

Go and Open the Door

Bethany Halford

What could be behind this door?
I'm wondering who else has hesitated.
I am.
Do I dare to touch?
Will I regret not doing it… or maybe doing it?
There could be the deepest, darkest, daring, loudest, quickest,
    saddest, happiest, nicest, greatest embrace
of nothing.

I'm opening the door… Oh.
I'm never doing that again.
Some doors are made to be closed.

An Average Day

Tim Justice

I open my eyes
and find myself on a heap of grass.
As I get up and glare into the distant fields
I see cows and sheep everywhere
their heads are down and tails turned high
so that they may be rid of their supper.
I look down and raise my arms.
My hands are larger than normal and my skin
is blue with a green texture of pouring water.
I stand tall and spread the dirt
far with a single step.
I look down to the sheep.
I laugh at the cows
once twice my height,
now the size of my thigh.

Counting Bruises

Caitlin Leach

I remember the satisfaction
Of holding his tiny pink nails
For the first time.
The first welcome home.

I remember the taste of sea air
After seven long years
Of longing for it
So desperately.

I remember laughing until
It hurt the butterflies
In my stomach.

I remember that one hurdle
Which shattered
My entire summer.

I remember sleeping on
Moth-bitten mattresses
After being forced
Out of my comfort zone.

I remember counting bruises
After playing 'yellow car'
On the journey home.

I remember the hair in the sink
After deciding to style my
Own fringe,
The shock on my mother's face.

I remember her tears on the
Crease of my thumb
After wiping away her sadness
And broken smiles.

I remember the scolding
And punishment
After giggling
At Nibbles' funeral.

I don't remember the hurt
But I remember feeling the scar
For the first time.

The Big Apple

Casey Todd Hall

I woke up and opened my eyes to see what looked like heaven.
Bright lights and a beautiful city, the Big Apple lay ahead of me.
Loud noises such as the yellow taxis' horns screeching through
the city.
Skyscrapers taller than the clouds surrounded by businessmen
and women.
Thousands upon thousands of photos snapped every second not
wanting to miss a thing.

'Have You Forgot Me?'

Emily Bond

Hushed voices
behind the curtain,
'Good luck' ringing
in my ears.

Adrenaline bursting
through my body
as we took
our final bow.

A warm glow
expanding
in my chest.

Tears of joy —
but also sadness.

It is over now.

The Black Sheep

Teresa Etheredge

The uncle I never met had a handlebar moustache
And a face like Johnny Depp
(Without the glasses).
He has a huge motorbike
And is never around.
Granny calls him the black sheep
But he never gave us any wool.

He always wanted to be a mechanic
So he wears grease-stained overalls
And pretends.

My uncle has huge bushy eyebrows
That he can lift independently
And four piercings in his left ear.
Every Christmas he sends a bunch of dead lilies and a bottle
    of wine

And photos of his dog.
A huge alsatian
Or maybe a rottweiler
That could rip out your throat in an instant.
He used to be a police dog
The best one ever

Who caught lots of murderers
And all forty thieves.

My uncle heard me tell the same jokes twice
And laughed every time.
He pushed me on the swings
And bought me secret chocolates.
I wish I'd met him.

Like in the Movies

Katie Cotton-Betteridge

I woke up and…
I remembered
what had happened
the night before.
I shivered
and got out of bed.
Wondering
thinking
afraid
I remembered…
I had been killed
and yet I woke up.
I had been killed,
and yet I remembered.
I had been killed,
and yet I could
shiver
wonder
think
feel fear
So I woke up, remembering.
shivering
wondering
thinking
afraid.
And I returned to my P.O.D.

My place of death.
In movies
it's what they do.
It's right
it gives answers.
And so I woke up
as though in a movie
where the right place
and the right answers
would be at the most wrong place.
Like in the movies.

My. Place. Of. Death.

Absence

Asraf Khan

Now that you are gone away
I search aimlessly for something to do.
The abundance of silence grips the house.
I watch TV as the sound echoes in the hollow passages.
I snack to my heart's content without the need to share
As the crumbs lie dormant for days to come
Three hundred men battle to defend against all of Persia.

Nummys Are Not Allowed in Hospitals

Colbie McKinnon

I remember the stale smell of disinfectant,
My mum grasping my tiny pale thumb,
The other wedged between my teeth.

I remember a room piled high with toys and Lego mountains
Layered with a snakes-and-ladders carpet.

I remember not knowing where I was or why,
The see-through tapes on my hand, white splodges in the middle,
Mum's concerned face and my gappy grin.

I remember the transportation on my magic bed.
I was in *Bedknobs and Broomsticks*,
Not quite grasping the concept of wheels.

I remember not moving, or not being able to move,
A sleepy sensation followed by no sensation.

I remember the knock of heels on concrete floor,
The realisation I was not cuddled in my *Bob the Builder* duvet,
Being offered jam sandwiches and refusing,
Yet wolfing down raspberry ripple ice cream.

I remember Nummys are not allowed in hospitals.

Fandoms

Meg Roberts

Well I woke up this morning
and I was in a Fantasyland.
Not Mordor, or Panem,
not even Wonderland.
I had not used a looking glass,
a shrinking drink,
or a growing cake.
I had not been given a token,
met Mr Waters,
or been told I am divergent.

Tea Bag Left In

Jessica Knight

A chair with frayed arms
A steady back
And a tarnished finish.

A tattered over-size jumper
With small grey buttons and holes to push your thumb through.

A cup of tea with the tea bag left in
A whirlpool of infusions
Warm and comforting
The taste of home.

A large blossom tree on the corner
With delicate flowers
And a large trunk.

Bournemouth

Tim Justice

On the weekend
We set off at eight
Just the four of us and a two-hour journey.
A moment of sickness and a grateful change of clothes.
We arrived to a full car park.
The sun blazed down as the waves flowed in.
An hour spent building castles,
Another on refreshments.
What seemed like two hours realistically was ten.
I could taste salt as I glared at a fading beach.
I can't wait till the end of this night.

Speed Cameras on Cleeve Hill

Teresa Etheredge

Speeding down
Being snapped on speed cameras
Ridiculous looks on our faces.

Swerving crazily
To avoid cars
Laughing at the ridiculous looks on their faces.

Reaching the bottom
Eyes sore from crying
Tyres squealing in indignation –
It was amazing.
We didn't do it again.

Listography

Bethany Halford

Did you know
Words don't hurt
Christmas is cancelled
Eloise is an opera singer
Squid is secretly pasta
The sky is both blue and not blue
Distance equals speed times time
Harry Potter isn't dead
But he's slowly dying
Like you.
Did you know –
You take pills to procreate
The equator doesn't exist
Zero isn't a number
I never procrastinate
Emily kicked my cat in the fire.

Did you know
Titanic makes me happy
Tomatoes are the main ingredients in orange juice
Celebrities aren't human
The queen is a secret spy... shhh don't tell anyone
England is the capital of London
I won the Hunger Games

Germany won the war
Water is bad for you
I failed my O.W.L.s.

Did you know
I'm related to Eddie the Eagle
And Cary Grant too
Snape couldn't cross the road.
I know God exists
History is about the future
I don't have anything I've had from a baby
It's illegal to cry
And lie.

Not What I Need

Jessica Knight

Now that you've gone away
I'll jump on each and every bed
And make as many cups of
Coffee as I want.
I'll stay awake all night
Even on Sunday.
I'll shower for hours.
But
Now you're gone
I'll do what I want
But not what I need.

My House

Casey Todd Hall

Running home from school, chucking my bag on the sofa,
Raiding the food cupboards for cookies and crisps,
Mum shouting, 'EAT SOME FRUIT!'
The TV blasting out Jeremy Kyle's annoying voice:
'Oi, this is *The Jeremy Kyle Show*, so listen!'
Sister screaming and running up and down the stairs.
Thinking in my head, 'Does she ever be quiet?'

Some of These Things Are True

Emily Bond

Blue seas are a lie.
Algebra is my favourite.

Babies come from seeds
that Mummy swallows
they grow
like a sunflower
in her tummy.

Tangerines are monkeys,
Brewster Bear was lots of fun,
Broccoli is a tiny tree
that multiplies inside you.

I will meet Prince Charming
when I'm twenty-three-and-a-half.

My great grandfather was a bigamist.

Punchline

Katie Cotton-Betteridge

Carefully calculating –
will it pay off?

Tone of voice
don't stutter
stumble
or talk too fast.

Is anybody listening?
The topic has moved on.
Oh, well.
I'll save that joke for another day.

A day when I'm not
the punchline.

Moony

Eloise Taylor

A forgotten chair
whose peels
represent tears.
A mouldy block
of cheese
cut square and sharp.
A beaten-up old truck
with rusty handles
and torn-up
leather seats.
Mandrakes
young and powerful
a symbol of pain.
A bathroom
equipped with
a secret chamber.
A haggard young man
who looks old
limping along
a cobbled path.
The wolf
with striking yellow eyes
and a hunger to kill.
An entry in a letter
or a map of sorts
waiting to cause mischief.

Seven Ways of Looking at Reflections

Bethany Halford

Into a person's eye
And seeing reflections.
Oh you are lost.

Impulses of ripples.
Water is beautiful, isn't it?
But then you see what it does.

Narcissistic,
I looked three times,
Turning it around.
You're gone.
Turning it back.

Nighttime, midnight, twilight
A window,
Beautiful scenery
Gone.
You look out and see the depths of your reflections.

Looking back,
Memories.
But you're only interested in the ones with…

The 'A' Was Once Removed

Colbie McKinnon

Trees bark, didn't you know?
And grass eats grass
Harry is also Daniel
Hogwarts is not real

Go and buy some elbow grease
We have none in the cupboard
Gandalf dies and Primrose lives

Dog's chocolate is not chocolate
And squid is really pasta
Teachers are people too

The sky is blue yet purple?
Black is the absence of colours
So lots of skies make black

The Earth floats on water
Zero is not a number
And zebras are made in China

The 'A' was once removed
While noses have no purpose
Money grows on trees
And people never lie

The Way Home Smiles

Caitlin Leach

I hear Dad sigh
The way he did when he scratched his forehead.
I hear Willow purr
The way she did when she clawed at the carpet on the stairs.
I hear the drain swallow water
The way it did when the basin was emptied.
I hear the plates clap against the table
The way they did when mum put out our tea.
I hear Holly thump down the stairs
The way she'd jump two at a time.
I hear Walle growl
The way he did when he craved attention
I hear Caden laugh
The way he did when his imagination took over.
I hear the kettle grumble
The way it did when guests came round.
I hear the click of a light switch.
Silence.

So You've Gone for Twelve Hours

Meg Roberts

So you've gone for twelve hours.
I'm all alone
left to my own devices.
I don't get dressed
pyjamas are comfier anyway.
I watch *Jeremy Kyle*
because I know you don't like him.
I eat an abundance of After Eights and chocolate.
Netflix my only friend.
I prance around the house
with my music way past six.
I sing at the top of my lungs until
that blue plastic tube is needed.
I ordered Chinese
and I don't need to wash up.
But now it's 8:55 and
I've less than five minutes left.

Longer Route

Asraf Khan

Surely this would lead to nowhere.
A small path swallowed by nature.
We pushed, battled our way in
The path closed behind us.
We took it in turns to lead.
The bushes bit and the stinging nettles stung,
Branches whipped back.
The evening sun crept through the gaps.
Being at the back is the worst.

The Authors

Emily Bond is a book fiend at heart, with a love of friends, fun and posh chocolate and a hate/hate relationship with maths. She writes from personal experiences, drawing on the details that make life memorable. Her favourite books combine humour and sadness in a way that feels honest and revelatory; she dreams of one day doing the same.

Katie Cotton-Betteridge is sixteen. Not entirely normal, but what does that matter? Eldest of four, she has a caring nature towards her younger siblings yet has always longed for an older brother or sister to protect her. She values family and friendship highly, and despite depression can be hyper and bubbly (sometimes a tad annoying). Obsessing over Harry Potter, with *Vampire Diaries* following closely, Katie can find the values of things despite child protagonists or supernatural overlays. She loves to write, and is currently working on a novel of her own. English literature, film nights, landscape photography are of large interest. Food-wise only overindulging in cookies, milk, spaghetti in tomato sauce, roast dinner sandwiches and strawberries matter. Quirky pink ends became turquoise, along a white blonde head which matches the punky theme she enjoys with the use of big-soled boots.

Teresa Etheredge is a doodling fifteen-year-old who does not enjoy Earl Grey tea. She was born one of eight children which suggests she is a pro at table football, arm-wrestling and Monopoly. This suggestion is probably correct. Teresa lives in

Cheltenham where she overindulges in ginger nuts, cucumber and laziness, carefully remembering to forget to do her homework. Later in life, after leaving Cambridge University (or possibly Buckingham Palace), she is expecting be an evil Snow White grandmother with seven cats, each named after a day of the week.

Bethany Halford You could use amiable to describe Bethany, but also arcane and brazen too. Bethany is a person consisting of many desires and passions, mostly being creative: things such as photography, writing, reading, choreographing and listening to music. Her poems express the many personalities and emotions that she expresses every day.

Tim Justice was born in England. With always an eye for new gaming gadgets and consoles, he's not an athlete but averagely built. A love and knowledge of films but with every year still more to learn. A true gamer but to many just another player. His main focus is campaign but sometimes he is drawn to multiplayer. He is a bit reclusive and when he leaves his house he does so for school or for journeys to the cinema.

Asraf Khan is the fifteen-year-old noblest prince of Canterbury ('Asraf' means 'noble prince'). Multiple ideas about multiple versions of himself in a new life in the sci-fi world would do nothing more than oblige. An overindulgence in cookies would never go amiss, intertwined with a heated discussion on the flavouring of pizza in the background! A responsible, loyal and caring friend, you could find no one like Asraf – he's prefect and house captain! His work tends to reflect his manic love for the supernatural/sci-fi, but who can complain with the ideas in this young man's head?

Jessica Knight is the girl with the weird orange hair and a subconscious wiggle. Her apparent taste for shapes and her coffee-shot chocolates gives her mind its inspiration. Her music is not music but her loveable approach is one that ensures your safety. She likes a good giggle, but when it comes to writing she's in a world of her own.

Caitlin Leach doesn't like a lot. But not many fifteen year olds do. Well, she does like cats. But cats don't like her. Caitlin is fond of tea and literature, but not all tea, and not all literature. She has a sponge for a brain, but still can't do maths or remember the difference between affect and effect. She has a really short attention span, hence the really short biogra

Colbie McKinnon is a social butterfly who has a thirst for knowledge and porridge. She has an accent, but only on certain words, for example, gone. Colbie spends her time escaping into distant and non-existent worlds such as Middle Earth and Hogwarts, and occasionally Central Perk. Colbie is fifteen years old and lives off Biscoff, marshmallow fluff and puppy cuddles.

Meg Roberts is a sixteen-year-old girl, a Hamleteer. She is lively, eccentric and a *Hunger Games* fanatic, though Super-wholock is on a close par. She is a Shakespeare queen who lives by the quote from *A Midsummer Night's Dream*: 'Though she be but little, she is fierce.' She lives by the queen himself, Ru Paul. Finally, Meg is the type of girl who will contentedly spend her Sundays in bed, with Ben & Jerry's cookie dough ice cream, having a Netflix binge.

Eloise Taylor is very stubborn and seemingly always right. Tends to disagree with people. Quirky and likes Marmite. Loves to read – no matter the genre. Always searching for that happy ending. Seen rough and tumble but yet not harmed by frivolous matters. Trustworthy and funny – you will laugh with her, not at her.

Casey Todd Hall is a fourteen year old going on forty. Overly obsessed with YouTube, sci-fi and the art of moaning, he puts a lot of his thoughts regarding these into his work. A big bowl of sarcasm and pasta make for his favourite dish – as long as he has a phone in his hand, cookies on a plate and wifi to boot. Taller than even some year 12s, he really is a BFG!